For my family across time,
with love and gratitude always
—M.R.R.

THIS IS A BORZOI BOOK PUBLISHED BY ALFRED A. KNOPF

Text copyright © 2024 by Mariana Ríos Ramírez
Jacket art and interior illustrations copyright © 2024 by Sara Palacios

All rights reserved. Published in the United States by Alfred A. Knopf, an imprint of
Random House Children's Books, a division of Penguin Random House LLC, New York.

Knopf, Borzoi Books, and the colophon are registered trademarks of Penguin Random House LLC.

Visit us on the Web! rhcbooks.com

Educators and librarians, for a variety of teaching tools, visit us at RHTeachersLibrarians.com

Library of Congress Cataloging-in-Publication Data is available upon request.
ISBN 978-0-593-56836-1 (trade) — ISBN 978-0-593-56837-8 (lib. bdg.) — ISBN 978-0-593-56838-5 (ebook)

The text of this book is set in 14-point Moranga Light.
The illustrations were created using handprinted gouache backgrounds, cut paper, and Adobe Photoshop.
Editor: Gianna Lakenauth | Designer: Taline Boghosian | Copy Editor: Artie Bennett
Managing Editor: Jake Eldred | Production Manager: Melissa Fariello

MANUFACTURED IN CHINA   10 9 8 7 6 5 4 3 2 1   First Edition

Abuelita's Gift

❁ A Día de Muertos Story ❁

written by

Mariana Ríos Ramírez

illustrated by

Sara Palacios

Alfred A. Knopf

New York

Julieta peeked inside the ofrenda boxes. Her eyes twinkled with the sight of La Catrina and papel picado.

"Is Abuelita *really* coming home?" Julieta asked.

"Yes!" Mamá replied. "Our ancestors' souls will visit us on Día de Muertos."

Julieta beamed. She couldn't wait for Abuelita's arrival.

Julieta and her siblings helped set up the ofrenda.

"What are *these*?" Mario asked.

"Mementos," Julieta answered. "To tell stories about our ancestors, so we always remember them."

Papá picked up a spool of burgundy thread.

"Your Bisabuela Cuca loved sewing dresses."

"And this?" Mario asked.

"Abuelito José was a pilot," Lola replied.

As Julieta listened, she had an idea.
She'd find a special gift for Abuelita.
One to make her smile, and show how
much she was missed.

Julieta recalled moments with Abuelita. She remembered Abuelita's wrinkled hands lacing delicate flowers into crowns they'd wear, pretending to be princesses. "That's it!" Julieta squealed.

She tried weaving a crown, but . . .

As she put away the flowers, Julieta heard chirping out the window. It reminded her of bird-watching with Abuelita.

"That's it!" Julieta squealed.

She tried folding an origami bird, but . . .

Julieta felt lost. With Día de Muertos around
the corner, she was running out of time and ideas.

Deep down, Julieta knew that what she and Abuelita loved most was dancing. They'd stomp their feet to the rhythm of jaranas, and sway their dresses side to side like ocean waves.

Dancing together created a world of their own. One filled with warmth and joy.

Julieta's eyes teared up as
another memory came to mind.

The day she stopped dancing
and packed everything away.

Without Abuelita, twirling to
"La Bamba" wasn't fun anymore.

When Julieta woke up on November first, she *still* hadn't found the right gift.

The whole family was busy preparing for the celebration. Mamá and Tía Yolanda made mole and tamales. Papá and Tío Paco rehearsed "La Llorona."

Her cousins and siblings made a marigold path
to guide souls to the ofrenda.

Everyone had found a way to
honor their ancestors,
except Julieta.

Julieta gazed at her ancestors' portraits, wondering about their stories. But when she noticed Abuelita's, something wasn't right.

Why aren't you smiling, Abuelita?

Julieta looked outside and noticed a girl and her abuela passing by with a shopping bag.

Julieta recalled her trips with Abuelita to La Feria de Día de Muertos. They'd buy calaveritas and Abuelita's favorite, dulces de leche.

"That's it!" Julieta squealed. "Lola!"

La Feria de Día de Muertos vibrated with colors.
Candies, chocolates, and calaveritas mesmerized visitors.
La música and the joyful hum of the crowd created a
festive mood. But for Julieta and Lola, it didn't feel as
magical without Abuelita.

And when they arrived at Doña Carmen's,
dulces de leche were sold out.

Once back home, Julieta sat by the ofrenda.
"I really tried," she cried. "You don't look like the Abuelita
I remember. Your smile . . . always made me smile."

"I'll fix this," Julieta said.

Julieta rushed upstairs. Holding her breath, she opened her memory box. Inside she found dance shoes, a lace fan, hair combs, and photos.

"That's my Abuelita!" Julieta said.

"You smiled the brightest when we danced."

Julieta closed her eyes and twirled.

In that moment, she felt
Abuelita dancing next to her.
"That's it!" Julieta whispered.

Later, the celebration began.
Julieta and her family enjoyed
arroz, mole, and pan de muerto.
Like always, the grown-ups told
stories about ancestors.
But this time, Julieta offered
a surprise of her own.

"Dancing was Abuelita's gift to me," Julieta said.
"Now, it's mine for us both."
    As her family cheered, Julieta tapped and waved
her dress. She'd found the perfect gift within herself.

With every twirl, she felt as if Abuelita's hands held hers.
And in her heart, Julieta knew as long as she danced,
her bond with Abuelita would live on forever.

Author's Note

Dear Reader,

Thank you for joining Julieta in this story about endless love and connection with Abuelita. I hope you enjoyed it and that it made you curious about your own ancestors. It's always interesting to learn more about where we come from to better understand who we are. When I wrote this story, I didn't intend it to be a guide on how Día de Muertos is celebrated. *Abuelita's Gift* is a fictional story that happens on Día de Muertos, but it's mostly a story about a girl who misses her abuelita and how she finds a way to feel close to her after she has passed away.

In Mexico, Día de Muertos is a unique and beautiful tradition. What fascinates me most is that instead of it being a time to mourn our dead loved ones, it's an opportunity to honor their lives and remember them with joy. For me, it's a pleasure to share with you glimpses of the culture and folklore that surround this wonderful tradition.

Although there are some common elements in how people celebrate Día de Muertos, like setting up ofrendas or visiting cemeteries, there's no right or wrong way to live this tradition. It depends on each family and the way they like to commemorate it from generation to generation. Within Mexico, the traditions and customs differ by region, according to the influence of pre-Hispanic cultures in the area, which explains the variety of ofrenda setups and festivities. Some families might have influence from different regions according to their ancestors' origins, while there might be others that don't set up ofrendas or celebrate at all. In addition, there are people who believe the souls of their deceased loved ones come visit temporarily; while others just focus on honoring and remembering them. For these reasons, the most important thing to keep in mind is that Día de Muertos is about love and family, and how we're all connected to our ancestors. As long as you get to know about them and remember their lives, the bond with your past will live on forever.

Warmly, Mariana

Glossary

abuelita: an endearing term for a grandmother, or abuela.

abuelito: an endearing term for a grandfather, or abuelo.

arroz: rice.

bisabuela: great-grandmother.

calaverita: a traditional skull made of sugar or chocolate and decorated with colorful icing and sequins.

La Catrina: a female skeleton in an elegant dress and hat, which has become one of the most recognizable symbols of Día de Muertos. The male counterpart of La Catrina is called El Catrín.

Día de Muertos: Day of the Dead in Mexico is a traditional celebration in different regions of the country, in which families honor and remember the lives of their deceased loved ones, who are believed to come back for a temporary visit on November 1 (children) and 2 (adults). Originally a pre-Hispanic celebration, it was later syncretized with Christian beliefs brought to Mexico by Spanish conquistadors. Nevertheless, Day of the Dead isn't the same as the Christian celebration of All Saints' Day or All Souls' Day, although they share the same dates and both remember the dead.

dulces de leche: soft sweets made from milk and sugar, similar to fudge.

Feria de Día de Muertos: an annual market in which vendors sell traditional calaveritas, crystallized fruits, catrinas, clay figures of skeletons, and other handcrafts related to Día de Muertos.

jarana: an eight-string guitar-like instrument from Mexico used to play music, like "La Bamba."

mole (MOH-lay): a traditional thick sauce usually served over chicken or meat. Mole poblano is one of the most popular varieties in Mexico and has chili peppers, nuts, and chocolate as some of its main ingredients.

música: music.

ofrenda: an offering placed on a home altar set up by families to remember and honor their ancestors on Día de Muertos. The set of an altar and the offering is also known as ofrenda.

pan de muerto: a traditional soft bread sprinkled with sugar made to celebrate Día de Muertos. Its circular shape represents life's cycle. The bone-shaped figures on its top symbolize the dead and the tears shed for them. The circle in the center represents a skull.

papel picado: colorful tissue paper flags tied together and chiseled with images related to Día de Muertos.

tía: aunt.

tío: uncle.

Ofrenda

Ofrenda Elements

Calaverita

represents those who have died and symbolizes that death is part of life

Candles

light the way to the ofrenda, represent the element fire

Cempasúchil flowers (marigolds)

guide souls to the ofrenda through color and scent

Favorite foods

to honor those who've died and to make them happy

Fruits of the season

food for the souls, represents the element earth

Glass of water

eases the thirst of the souls after their journey, represents the element water

Incense

cleanses the atmosphere

Pan de muerto

food for the souls, represents the cycle of life and death

Papel picado

sets a cheerful tone, represents the element air

Personal objects

to remember the lives of dead loved ones

Petate (puh-TAH-tay)

a woven bedroll so that the souls can rest after their journey

Photographs

to show who is being honored in the ofrenda

Salt

purifies the souls